ELI and His Little White LIE

By Goldie Golding

Drawings by Linda Snowden

Airbrush color by Michael Horen
at ArtScroll Studios

"I didn't do it," said Adina.
"It wasn't me," said Shani.
"Nor me," said Yossi.
"Then who ate the chocolate pudding cake?" asked Shani.
"What chocolate pudding cake?" said Eli.

But there was chocolate all over Eli's face, and even on his shirt. He *did* eat it!
Eli should have told the truth.
But he didn't.

All of a sudden something flew onto Eli's shoulder. He tried to brush it away with his hand.

"Shoo, fly," he said.

"I'm not a fly," a voice answered.

"*Who* said that?" asked Eli, looking all around.

"*I* didn't hear anything," said Shani.

But Eli was able to hear it.
And Eli was able to see it.
It was little, it was fluffy, and it was white.
Eli picked it up and held it in the palm of
his hand.
"If you're not a fly," said Eli, "then what
are you?"
"Just a little white lie," it said.
"I think you're cute," said Eli.

Eli loved the little white lie.
He took it with him everywhere.

He took it to the park,

he took it
to the store,

and he even
took it to school.

One day Shani found a ball.
"Is this yours?" she asked Eli.
"Uh huh," said Eli and he nodded yes.
He knew that it wasn't his.
Eli should have told the truth.
But he didn't.

All of a sudden the little white lie began to grow! And then . . .

It changed from white to pink!

"Let's play," said the pink lie to Eli when it stopped growing.
"I can't play," said Eli. "I have to do my homework."
"You can do it later," the lie said. "Come."
And it held out its pink fluffy arm to Eli.
Eli and the pink fluffy lie played for a long time.

Eli came home late.

"I'm glad you're home," said Eli's mother. "It's almost suppertime. Do you have any homework to do?"

"I don't think so," said Eli.

He *did* have homework to do. Eli should have told the truth. But he didn't.

All of a sudden the lie began to grow again!
It grew bigger and bigger. And then . . .

It changed from pink to blue!

"Let's play king," said the blue lie when it stopped growing. "I'll be the king and you'll be my slave. Now bring me something to eat."

"I don't like this game at all," Eli complained. "And I don't even like you anymore!"

Then Eli did a very bad thing. He threw a plate down to the floor. Crash! It smashed into tiny bits.

Eli's mother ran quickly into the room.
"What happened?" she asked.
"The plate fell off the table," Eli said.
"It wasn't my fault."
Eli should have told the truth.
But he didn't.

As soon as he told this lie, the big blue lie began to grow even bigger.
It grew, and it grew, and it grew!

And then
POOF!

It changed from blue to purple!
Soon it became a gigantic . . .
ugly . . . disgusting . . . purple lie!
Now the lie took Eli wherever *it*
wanted to go.

"I'm hungry," growled the ugly purple lie.
What's for dinner?"
"Spaghetti and meatballs," replied Eli.
"It's my favorite dish."
"Mine too," said the ugly purple lie and it
gobbled up everything that was in the pot!

Eli was upset. He ran to his room and shut the door. He leaned against the door to keep the lie out.

"Go away," said Eli. "I don't like you anymore!"

But the purple lie didn't listen. It pushed the door open.

Next, Eli tried stuffing the purple lie into the
broom closet. But it didn't fit.

Then he tried pushing it under the couch. But the couch popped up to the ceiling with Eli on it.

"Oh, it's no use," sobbed Eli. "You just won't go away!"

Finally Eli said, "I'm going to sleep.
Maybe when I wake up, you'll be gone."
Eli said *Shema* and went to bed.
The purple lie fell asleep in the rocking chair.
It made loud and funny snoring sounds.

That night Eli dreamed about his lie.
"I used to think you were so cute when
you were little and white," said Eli.
"How did you *ever* grow into something
so ugly and big and purple?"
"Because you kept lying," said the lie.
"But now I want you to go away!" Eli
shouted.

"Do you really want me to leave?" asked the lie.

"Yes, I *truly* do!" screamed Eli. And he suddenly woke up from his sleep.

Now Eli finally knew how to get the horrible creature to go away.

"I'm sorry that I ever told that first little lie," Eli said. "Now I know why the Torah says:

מִדְּבַר שֶׁקֶר תִּרְחָק.

Keep far away from lies!

From now on, I will always tell the truth!"

And he did.
That morning, when Eli sat down to
breakfast, his mother asked, "Eli, did you
wash your hands?"
Eli was about to lie. But he didn't.
Instead, he told the truth.
"I didn't wash yet, Mommy. I'm sorry.
I'll do it right now."
Mother gave Eli a big
hug and kiss.

As soon as Eli told the truth, the gigantic, ugly, purple lie started to shrink!
"Why are you getting smaller?" asked Eli.
"Because you are telling the truth," it said.

Then Eli told his brother and sisters that *he* was the one who ate the chocolate pudding cake. Eli felt much better now.

When the lie heard Eli telling the truth again, it packed its bags and it got ready to leave.

Eli smiled as he watched the lie shrink
smaller and smaller and smaller.
And then . . .

It was gone.

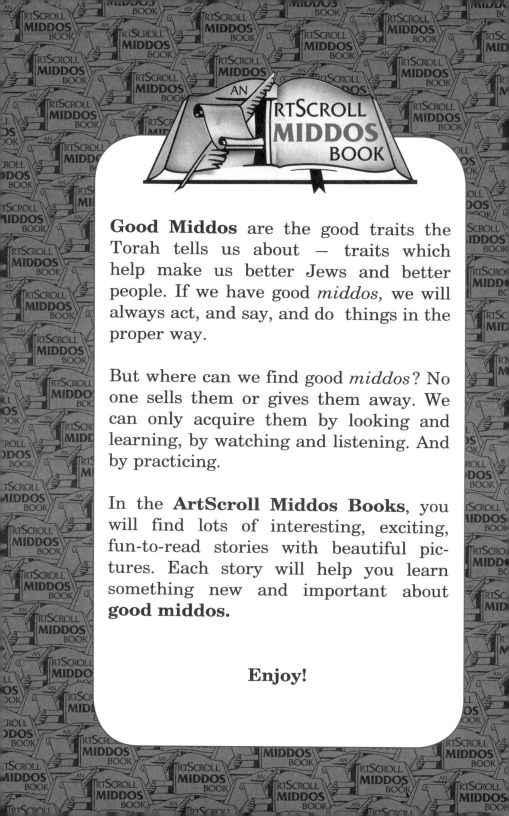

AN ArtScroll MIDDOS BOOK

Good Middos are the good traits the Torah tells us about — traits which help make us better Jews and better people. If we have good *middos,* we will always act, and say, and do things in the proper way.

But where can we find good *middos*? No one sells them or gives them away. We can only acquire them by looking and learning, by watching and listening. And by practicing.

In the **ArtScroll Middos Books**, you will find lots of interesting, exciting, fun-to-read stories with beautiful pictures. Each story will help you learn something new and important about **good middos.**

Enjoy!